BRICK

A

B

C

BRICK PALS

The ABC letters and the scenes for each letter were built with LEGO® bricks and were photographed by Brick Pals.

LEGO®, the brick configuration, and the minifigure are trademarks of The LEGO Group, which does not sponsor, authorize, or endorse this book.

CreateSpace Independent Publishing Platform

Copyright © 2013 Brick Pals

ISBN: 1484047966

ISBN-13: 978-1484047965

Aa Bb Cc Dd Ee

Ff Gg Hh Ii Jj

Kk Ll Mm Nn Oo

Pp Qq Rr Ss Tt

Uu Vv Ww

Xx Yy Zz

Big **A**, little **a**,

What words start with **a**?

An alligator is catching an **airplane**.

An **arrow** is pointing the way.

An **ambulance** is going to the rescue.

Ants are climbing on an **apple** tree.

How many **apples** are on the tree?

Big **B**, little **b**,

What words start with **b**?

Blue, **brown**, **black**,

boy, **ball**, **bat**, **backpack**,

building, **bin**, **bridge**, **brick**,

banana, **broom**, **bicycle**, **book**,

bird, **binocular**, **bush**, **box**,

bench, **boat**, and **bus**.

So many words **begin** with **b**.

How many **balloons** do you see?

Big **C**, little **c**,

What words start with **c**?

A **cat** is on a **cow**.

A king wears a **crown**.

A **camel** is beside a **castle**.

A **clock** has the shape of a **circle**.

A **chef** is roasting **chicken**.

The smell even attracts the **crocodiles**.

What else begins with **c**?

Point at the picture as you see:

cactus, camera, car, carrot, chain, chair, chimney, cone, cup

Big **D**, little **d**,

What words start with **d**?

Door, **driver**, and **doctor**.

A girl is having an "adventure".

What **does** she **dream** about?

Dog, **duck**, **dragon**, and **dinosaur**.

How many **dinosaurs** do you see?

Big **E**, little **e**,

What words start with **e**?

Point at the picture as you see:

elephant, eagle, entrance, eye, ear, eight

Big **F**, little **f**,

What words start with **f**?

Fish, **food**, **fruit**,

face, **fountain**, **flag**,

fire, **fence**, **flower**, and **frog**.

Number **four** and number **five.**

The **firefighter** is brave!

Big **G**, little **g**,

What words start with **g**?

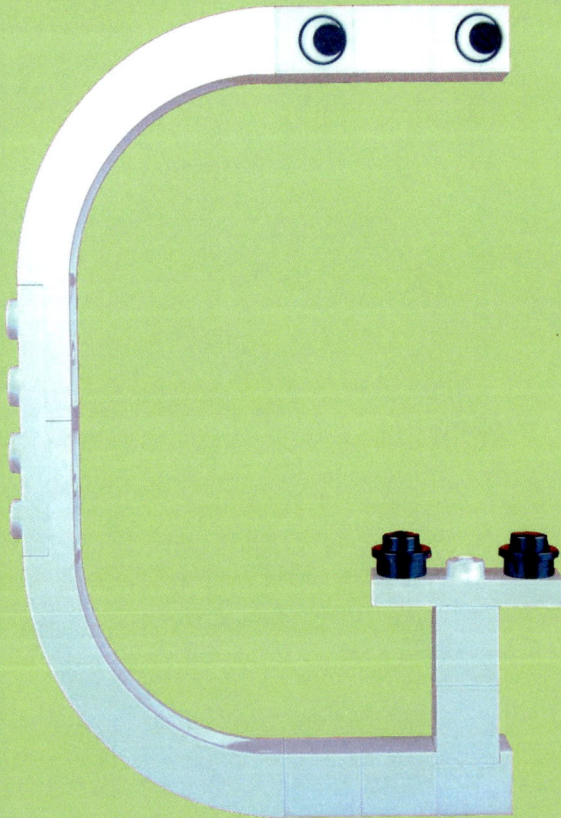

Green, **gray**, **grass**,

garbage truck, **gate**, **glass**,

gas, **girl**, **gift**,

gorilla, **giraffe**, and **goat**.

Big **H**, little **h**,

What words start with **h**?

Head, **hair**, **hat**, **hunter**,

handle bar, **hand**, **hammer**,

hill, **hook**, **horse**, **helmet**,

house, **hospital**, and **helicopter**.

Big **I**, little **i**,

What words start with **i**?

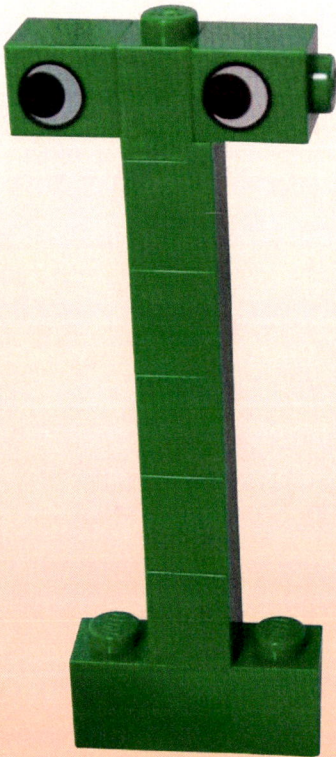

Ice cream **is** what **I** want,

— after traveling **in** a hot summer day.

Sitting by the **ivy**.

Resting in an **inn**.

Dreaming how comfortable and cool **it**
will be —

if I can live in an **igloo**.

Big **J**, little **j**,

What words start with **j**?

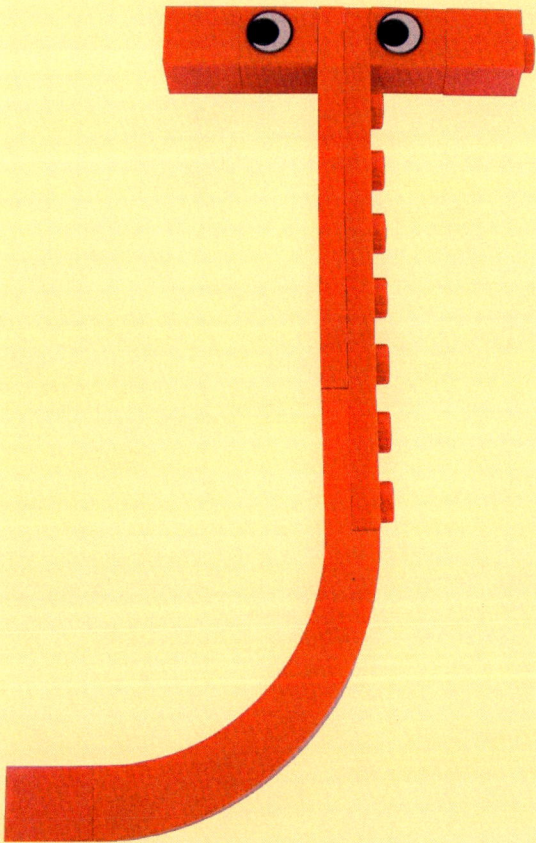

A man is wearing a **jacket**.

Jewelry is what he wanted.

Can the **jellyfish** fit in the **jar**?

I don't think so, do you?

Jet, **jeep**, and **jump** rope.

The **jogger** keeps his body in good shape.

Big **K**, little **k**,

What words start with **k**?

A **keyboard** in the **kitchen**.

A **king**, holding a **key**.

What animals do you see?

Koala, **kitten**, and **kangaroo**.

Do you like them as much as I do?

Big **L**, little **l**,

What words start with **l**?

Leaf, **lamp**, **letter**, **leg**,

lion, **ladder**, and **log**.

A **lady** is using her **laptop**.

The **ladybug** is **larger** than the **lock**.

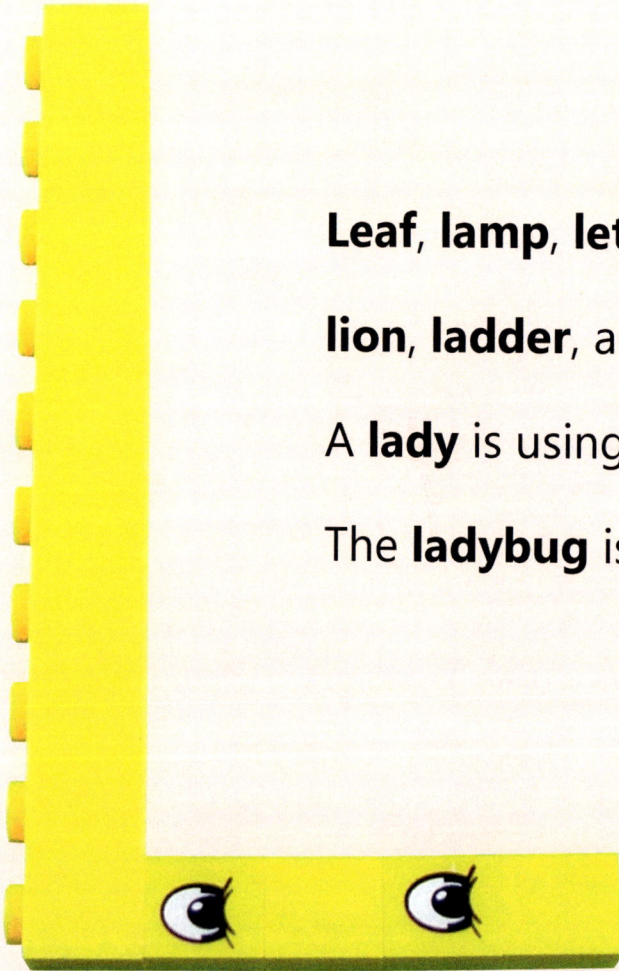

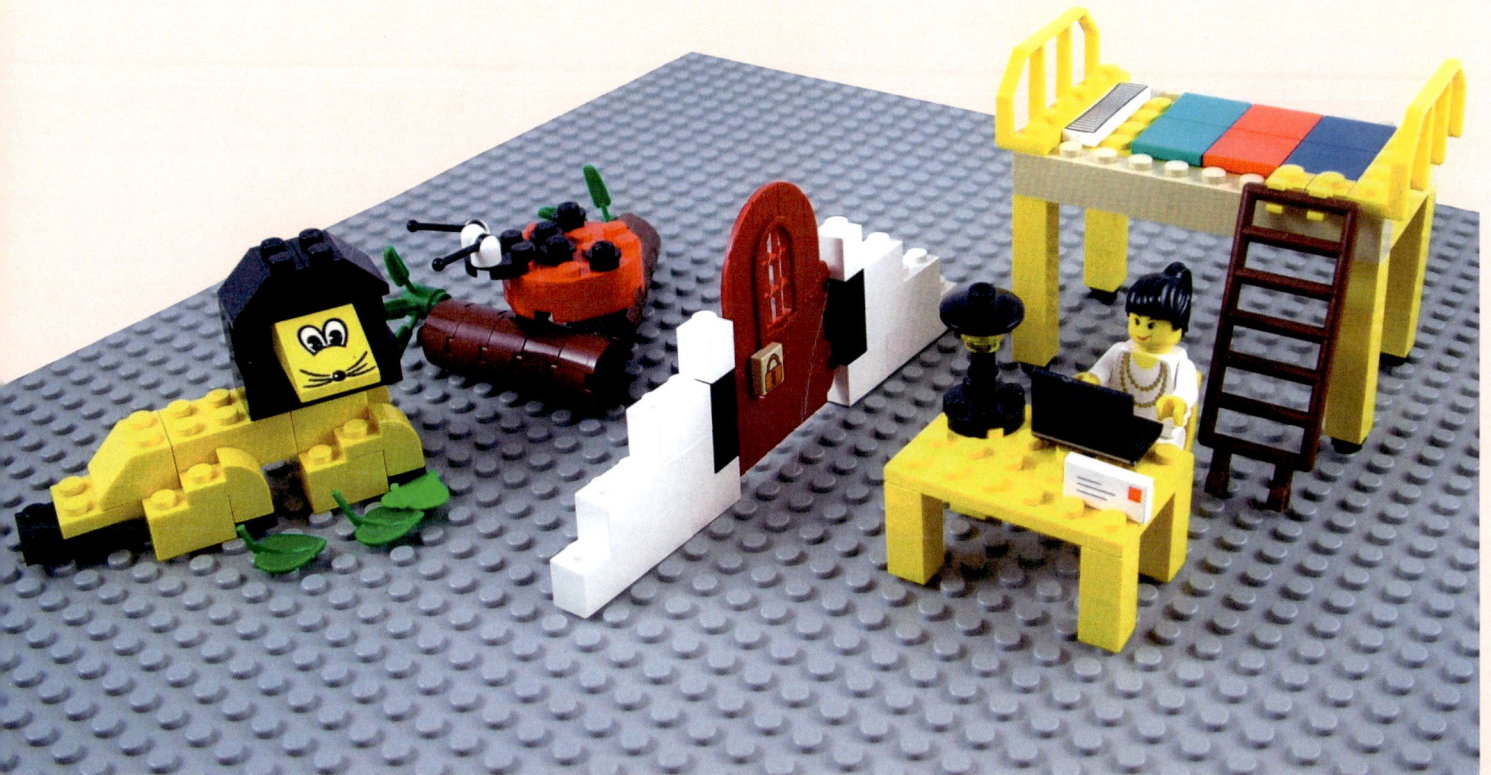

Big **M**, little **m**,

What words start with **m**?

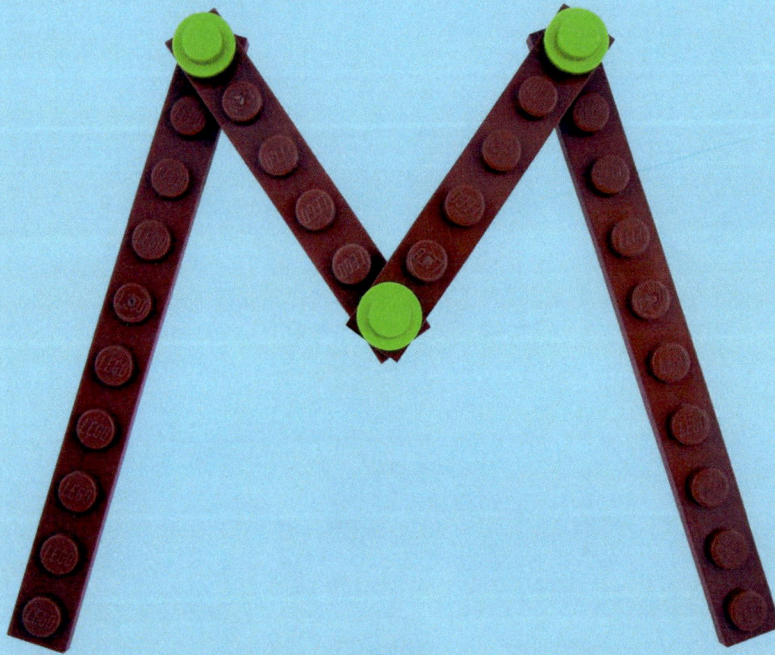

magnifying glass, money, mountain, motorcycle, mail, mirror, map

One **man**, two **men**, and three **men**.

One **mouse**, two **mice**.

One **monkey**, two **monkeys**.

Do you see the difference?

Big **N**, little **n**,

What words start with **n**?

Net , **nose**, and **nest**.

The **number nine** starts with **n**.

A map shows **north** the direction.

Big **O**, little **o**,

What words start with **o**?

Oil, **octopus**, **oar**,

one, **orange**, and **owl**.

Big **P**, little **p**,

What words start with **p**?

Pink, **purple**, and **people**.

The **penguin** is adorable.

Police, **plate**, and light **pole**.

Presents are the best of all.

Pan, **propeller**, and **pilot**.

Pizza is my favorite.

Can you find a **piano** and a **pen/pencil**

holder somewhere in this book?

Big **Q**, little **q**,

What words start with **q**?

What is a **quarter** of a circle?

What is the **question** in the **quiz?**

Can you get the answer **quickly**?

Tell the **queen quietly**.

Big **R**, little **r**,

What words start with **r**?

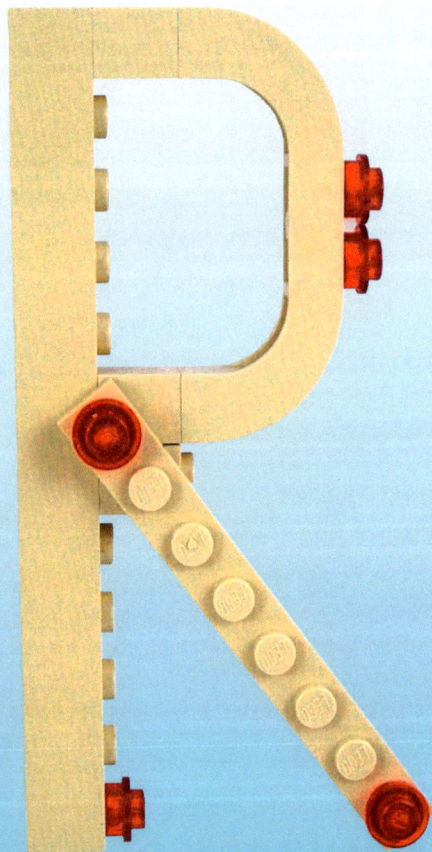

Rake, **race**, **ramp**,

rat, **rope**, and **robot**.

Is there a **roof** above the **room**?

Do not let the **rocks** block the **road**.

Can you find a **river** in this book?

Big **R**, little **r**,

What color starts with **r**?

Red, orange, yellow, green, blue, and purple.

Rainbows are beautiful!

Big **S**, little **s**,

What words start with **s**?

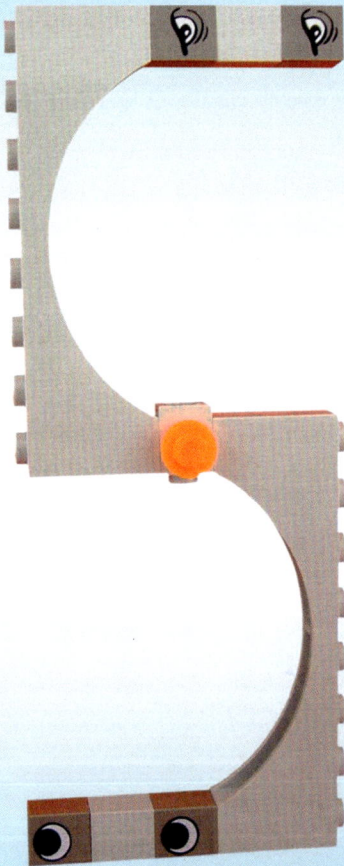

I like to **swing** and **slide** in the play ground,

with **Santa** and **snowman** around.

Christmas is always my favorite **season**.

Waiting for my presents in **Santa's sleigh**, and under the Christmas tree.

Soccer, **surfing**, **skating**, and **skiing**.

What **sports** do you play?

What else **starts** with **s**?

Point at the picture as you **see**:

six, seven, shark, spider, snake, scorpion, shell, shovel, stair, star, store, suitcase, stop sign

Big **T**, little **t**,

What words start with **t**?

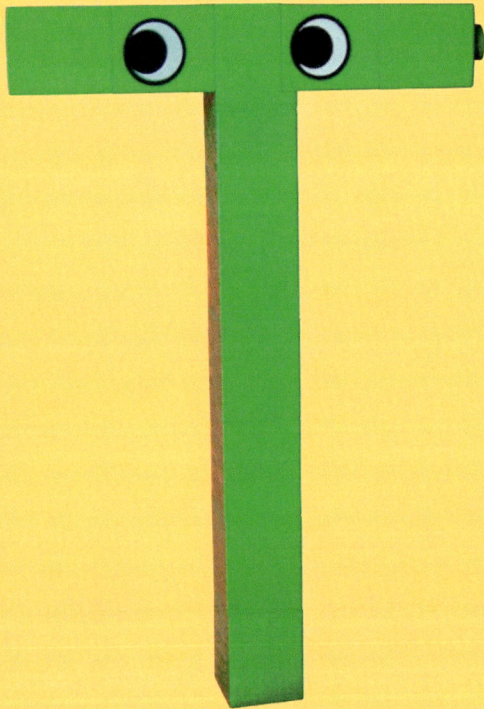

Triangle, **tricycle**,

time, **telephone**, **table**,

TV, **trophy**, **tow truck**,

train, **tower**, and **tail**.

What else begins with **t**?

Point at the picture as you see:

two, three, ten, twelve, twenty one
tire, torch, tree trunk, T-shirt

Big **U**, little **u**,

What words start with **u**?

People are standing **upstairs**.

Some of them wear **uniforms**.

Flowers are **under** the platform.

Saying 'Welcome' to the **unicorn**.

An **umbrella** is **upside** down.

A **unicycle** is by the stairs.

I see a flag of the **United** States.

Big **V**, little **v**,

What words start with **v**?

Vest, **van**, **video** camera, **vacuum** cleaner,

and a **vase** with **violet** flowers.

Big **W**, little **w**,

What words start with **w**?

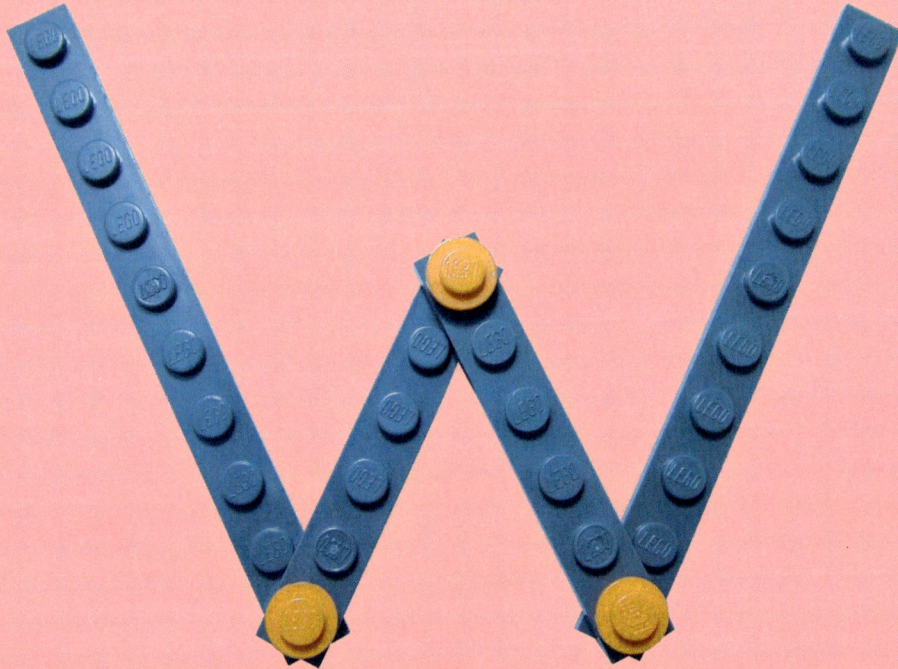

Watch, water, wall,

web, whip, well,

wheel, woman, window, wagon,

wrench, white, and watermelon.

Big **X**, little **x**,

What words start with **x**?

Playing the **xylophone** is fun.

The **X-ray** helps the doctor to heal a man.

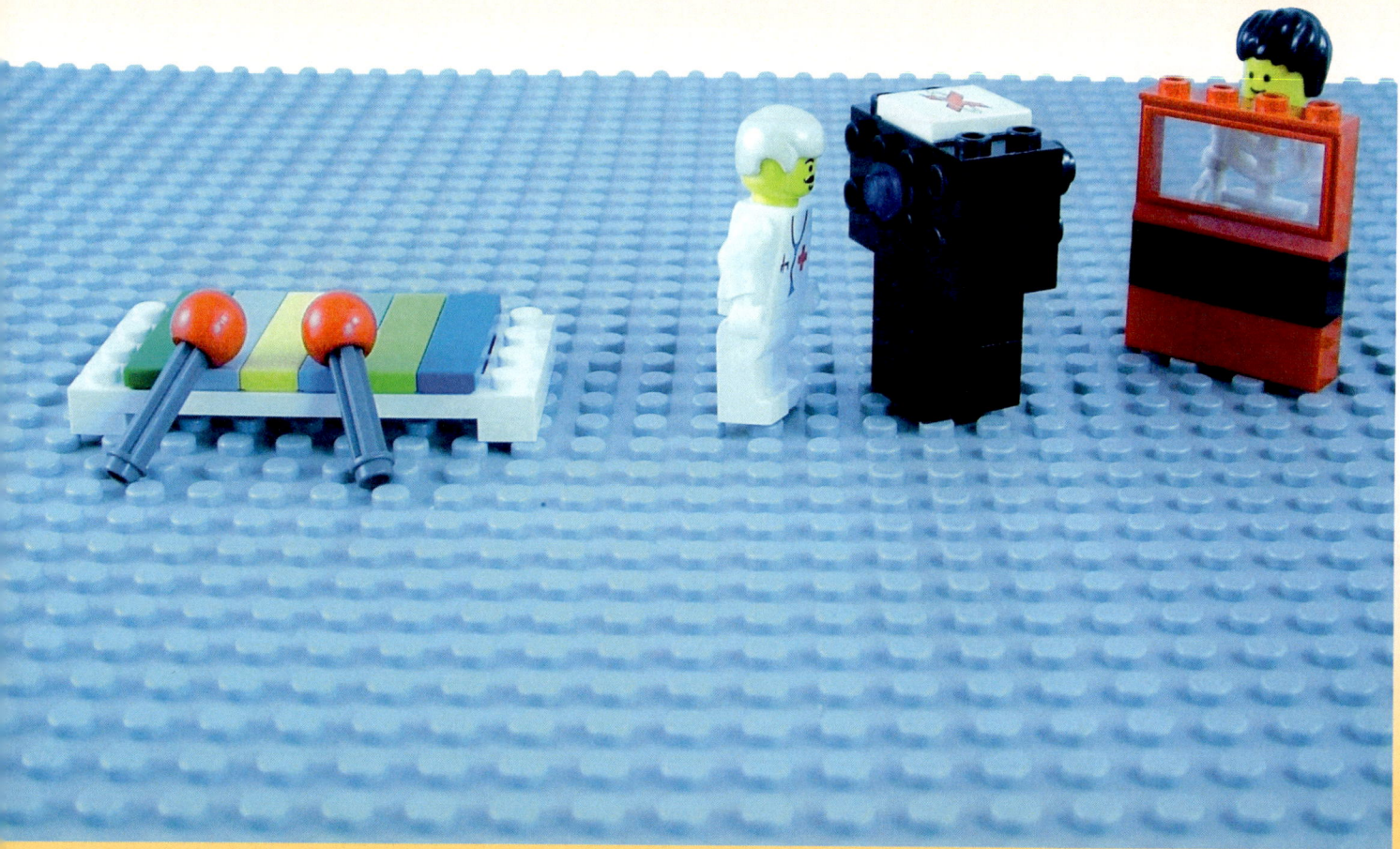

Big **Y**, little **y**,

What words start with **y**?

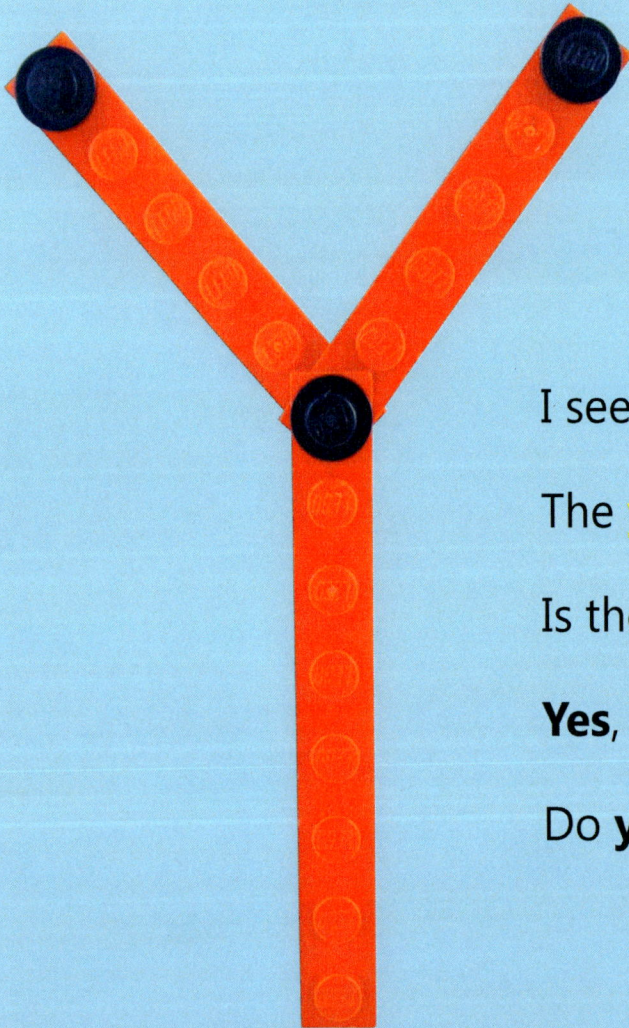

I see the yellow beak of a duckling.

The yellow flowers are blooming.

Is the **yard** beautiful?

Yes, I think so.

Do **you**?

Big **Z**, little **z**,

What words start with **z**?

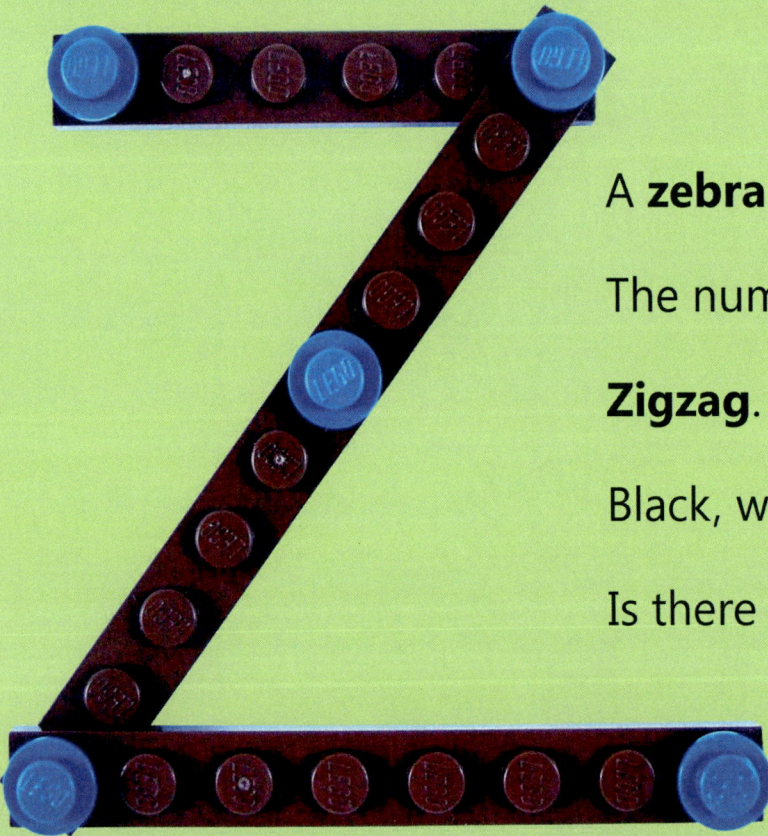

A **zebra** lives in the **zoo**.

The number **zero** starts with **z**, too.

Zigzag.

Black, white.

Is there a **zipper** also on your jacket?

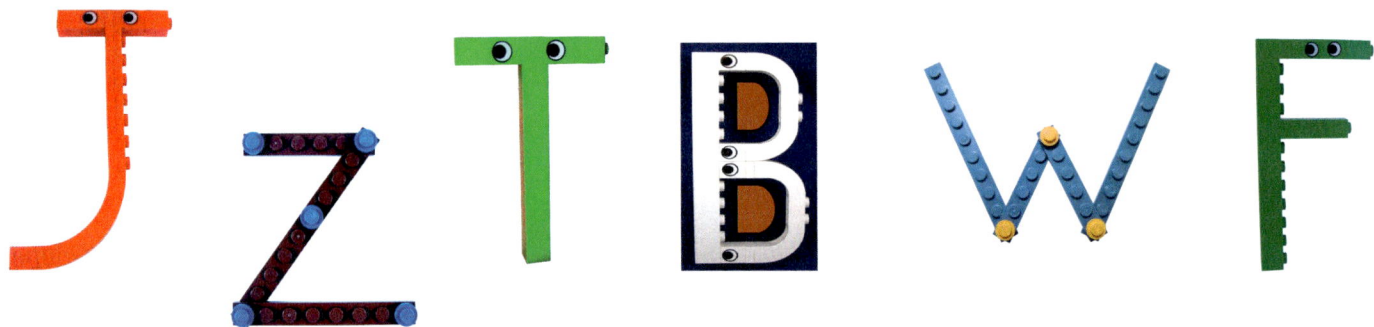
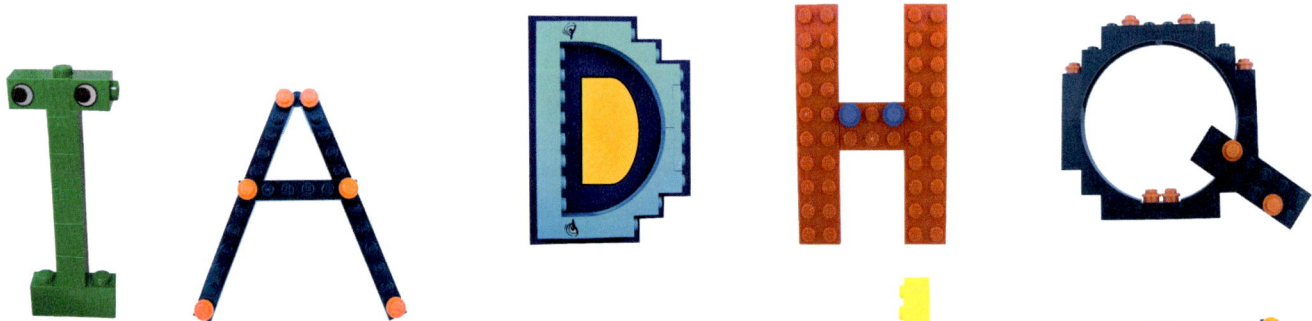

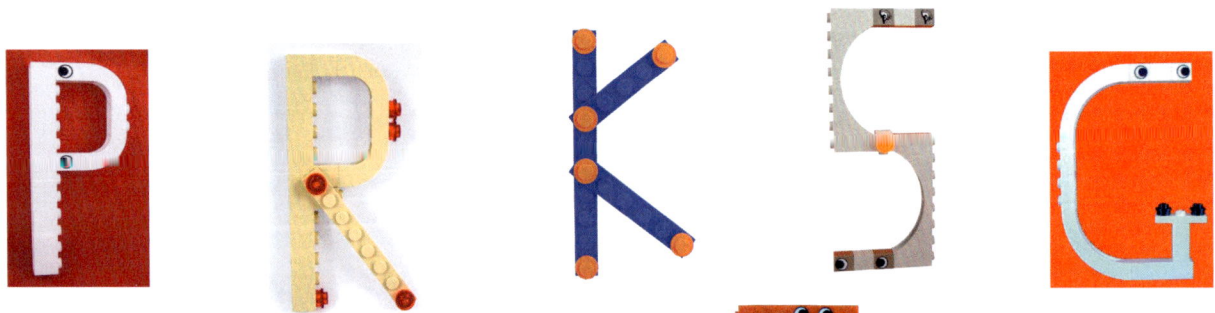
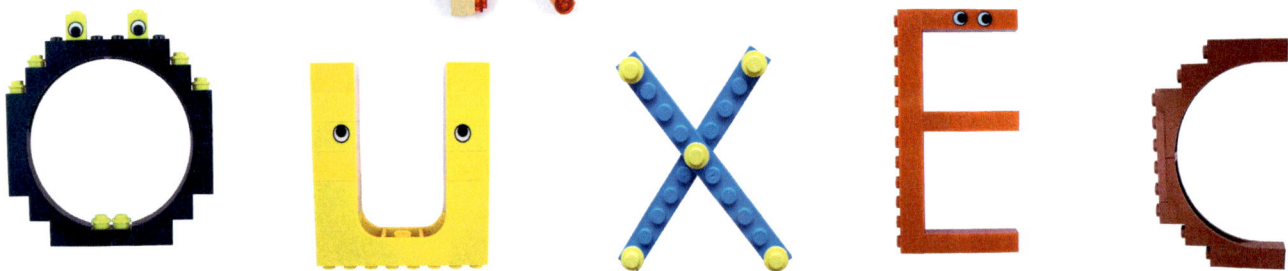

Made in the USA
San Bernardino, CA
26 November 2016